DATE DUE

AUG 29 2003

The
Ghost of Shanghai

The Ghost of Shanghai

Claude Guillot
ILLUSTRATED BY Fabienne Burckel

Harry N. Abrams, Inc., Publishers

B*aba* gets up before sunrise to be ready when Mr. Song arrives downstairs on his motorcycle. He wedges his bowl of noodles in the muffler so it will stay warm for breakfast later. Both of them are off to work in the huge underground pipes in another suburb of Pudong, to the east of Shanghai.

After *Baba* leaves, I watch Mrs. Ha Piou doing her Tai Chi exercises in her kitchen across the street. Although our building is not in the nicest neighborhood, our apartment is very comfortable. We have central heating (nice and toasty), city gas for the stove, and even running water. We are only on the fourth floor, so the water pressure is good.

CHILDREN'S ROOM

E
GUILLOT

CHILDREN'S ROOM

My name is Li, and I am my parents' only *nuer*. I would love to have a *didi* (even though boys can be a real pain), but that is not possible. The government does not advise families to have more than one child in China. And anyway, our apartment is already small for the three of us, even with the bathroom.

M ama folds up the roll-away couch where she and *Baba* sleep, stacks the blankets on the shelf, and gets out her equipment. The room is suddenly transformed into a dress shop! *Mama* has two plastic mannequins, a foreign sewing machine, and a pile of catalogues showing recent Hong Kong styles. *Mama* is a dressmaker. It is her true passion, although she must also work on the assembly line at a *gongchang* for extra money. She is very talented. Beautiful women come from very far away with special fabrics, asking her to make modern, fashionable *lifu* as well as traditional Shanghai costumes for ancient ceremonies.

While *Mama* begins her work, I roll up my sleeping mat, and arrange my notebook and pens on my little table because I have a long *xin* to write. I love being with *Mama* when I do not have school. I straighten the *hua* of my *gui* next to the television (which works only when it wants). The *hua* was done by a great artist. I have also seen my *gui*—he is a very nice ghost. But it is a strange story, which means I should start at the beginning.

★   ★   ★

I met my *gui* when Mrs. Ha, the wife of a rich rice merchant from Zhong-shan Lu, the commercial district next to Old Town, came to visit. She wanted my *Mama* to make a very special wedding *lifu* made of organdy and silk for her *nuer,* who deserved the very best. *Mama* and Mrs. Ha discussed the design, the length, the quality of the fabric, and the embroidered beads that would be used.

Soon after, the fabrics were delivered by a chauffeur in uniform. He really impressed Mrs. Suzu, our building superintendent. Mrs. Suzu is also our building busy body. It is difficult for her to watch us enjoy things she could not have when she was younger, so she always lets us know what she thinks about our lives. But even though she interferes in our business, we are happy she watches over us.

Mama would be at work on the *lifu* even before *Baba* left in the morning, busying herself with drawing, cutting, clipping, and sewing. Then off she would go to the *gongchang*. When she got back, she would pick up where she had left off and work late into the night. Before falling asleep, I would watch her turn and turn the rolls of cloth to the gentle clacking of the foot-powered sewing machine. As she sewed, *Mama* hummed the old songs of Lian Hua Lao quietly to herself.

One morning when I awoke, *Mama* was sweeping up the balls of cotton and silk strands which had fallen all around her work area. The sewing machine had been put away. On the counter, tied up in strong linen string, was the *lifu*, finally finished. *Mama* was very tired, but also relieved that the *lifu* was done.

"Li," she said, "I only have four days off from work this week, so you will need to borrow Mrs. Suzu's *zixingche* and deliver the *lifu* to the bride for her fitting. Please be very careful and pay attention—this *lifu* was a lot of work!"

The *zixingche* was stored next to the room where the coal was kept. A shrug of Mrs. Suzu's shoulder signaled permission for me to borrow it.

"Be careful," she said in a sharp tone. "This *zixingche* is very heavy, and if one is not careful, it can take off on its own. So pay attention."

I pedaled down Dragon Street along the canals, keeping Mrs. Suzu's words in mind. I was careful to sit up straight and not be distracted by the increasingly heavy traffic coming toward me. The chain rubbed loosely against the guard next to the pedals, producing a rhythmic backdrop for my gentle pace. Click clack, click clack, click clack . . . I began to wander off into the land of dreams.

Suddenly, a three-wheeled cycle crashed into me. A huge cargo of caged chickens flew toward me. The birds' eyes were big and round. There were more and more chickens, and then . . . nothing.

I did not feel a thing. Flat on my back, I watched the sun playing hide and seek with the watery clouds. I felt light. No more horns, bells, shouts, or other street racket. I was a wisp of cotton floating on the wind towards the sky.

T hen I saw my *gui*. He came and went in the light, a little bedraggled, his beard a mess and his brow knitted. His long red mandarin robe flapped in the cool breeze.

"Li, you are like me, little one," he said. "You have lost your way."

"No, no," I answered him. "I am fine. I am floating in the air. Who are you?"

"I am Master Chen," my *gui* said. He gently caressed my hair. Something warm ran down behind my ear. I clung to him.

"I am a little afraid," I said. In fact, I was very afraid when I noticed him try to hide my blood on his hand.

"Do not be afraid, little Li. I have the power to send you back from where you have come. In exchange, I will ask you to take the time to write a *xin* to my son, the oldest of the Chen of Canton clan. You must tell him of our meeting. He may not believe what you say, so do not forget to mention my ruby seal, hidden for all these years under the roots of the cedar bonsai I grew. Tell him not to water it too much." Then he kissed me in the hollow of my ear, and I felt his beard tickle my cheek. "Goodbye, Li," he said.

"Goodbye, Master Chen," I said. I was no longer afraid.

Abruptly, the street racket returned. A crowd had formed around me. When I looked up, I saw that the women in the salon across the street were staring in my direction in shock and wonder. When the salon owner noticed me lying in the street, she immediately came to help.

As the woman approached, I became more aware of what was happening around me.

"The *lifu*!" I said frantically. "And Mrs. Suzu's *zixingche*!"

"It's okay, *xiao peng you*," said the salon owner. "The *lifu* and the *zixingche* are both right here. You have been very brave." She helped me up and led me to the back of the salon, into her apartment.

I felt a little dizzy, so I was glad to sit in her living room and have some tea. She had many nice things, including a brand new game with little wooden figures that had to be turned in order to kick a ball. Until then, I had only seen one on TV. She must be very successful.

热爱五七汇水爱毛主偈

When I was able, I started on my way again, but this time more carefully than before. I walked for a while, pushing the *zixingche* through the Yu Garden, over the footbridges, and through the Tea Garden.

In Old Town, the crowd was overwhelming. I had a hard time wading through the groups of people practicing Tai Chi, the cages of animals on their way to the market, and even, behind Yu Yuan, the couples dancing to the clanking and jangling of party loudspeakers.

After walking my *zixingche* for more than an hour, I finally arrived at the Ha family residence in Fuxing Dong Lu. I was a little intimidated by the yards and passages that opened up before me behind the heavy, red-lacquered door (the biggest door I had ever seen!). The silence was so different from the infernal noise of the street.

A little girl named Yi helped me hide my *zixingche* behind the door. She was neighbors with the Ha family and knew their place well. She was free to walk around as she wished. Her cousin was playing with a huge flying beetle on the end of a string in the alleyway. Yi invited me to share a bowl of steamed *shuijiao* with her *Yeye* Tchou. Then she led me to a beautiful flower garden, filled with many different kinds of roses. In the arbor hung two bamboo cages, half-covered in blue polka-dotted fabric. And there were two yellow-beaked mynah birds. Walls were covered with glazed terra-cotta bricks portraying rows and rows of tiny trees populated by little clay farmers and fishermen.

As I ate the *shuijiao*, I told Yi and *Yeye* Tchou about my adventure that morning. Little by little, *Yeye* Tchou forgot about eating as he listened to my tale and sank deeper and deeper into his pear-tree chair.

"Come!" Yi whispered, pulling me by the sleeve. "Ignore him. He does that sometimes, usually when he thinks of the wars he was in. You should go and deliver your *lifu* now."

Yi led me through a dark alley. Then we passed over cobblestone yards linking buildings that used to be old stables, servants' quarters and kitchens. Finally we arrived at the vast courtyard of the family villa. Yi left me standing there alone, clutching my package tight against my chest. Dragons (with very scary faces) carved in glazed stone seemed ready to spring at me at any moment. Two stone dogs stood atop a stair. I wanted to run away as fast as I could.

A door opened and an old woman in a beautiful robe came towards me. She hobbled at a gait unexpected for someone her age. She looked as if she had lived during the time of the emperors. Very kindly, she led me to the lavish rooms where Mrs. Ha and her *nuer* were being bustled about by servants.

The rooms were filled with precious things I had never seen in Pudong. Dragon porcelains and golden brushes made me think of the school visit my class had once made to a museum. I also saw a hair dryer and an enormous TV made in Hong Kong.

Mrs. Ha smiled at me as she unwrapped the paper, revealing the *lifu*. I stood stiff in the entrance hall while all of the elegant ladies ooh-ed and ah-ed over the perfect handiwork of the modest factory worker from Pudong. I was proud of *Mama*, who had put her whole heart into the *lifu*. Mrs. Ha was overjoyed. She presented me with an envelope for *Mama*, and two *kuai* for me (I could buy pencils!) as she showed me to the door.

I was about to mount my *zixingche* when *Yeye* Tchou put his hand on my shoulder.

"*Xiao* Li," he said. "Do not leave right away, little plum!" He had a nervous smile and his jaw was clenched. "Your story truly touched me," he said. "You owe the spirit of Master Chen a great deal. He did you a very important favor. You should know that I also saw Master Chen on the Zhongshan Lu, where you had your accident this morning." He paused.

"It was many years ago," he continued. "Master Chen was known as a brave man. He would often come from Canton to take care of business in Shanghai. The jealous shop owners in Shanghai accused him of siding with the workers and encouraging strikes in their *gongchang*. It was not an easy time and the shop owners' businesses were at great risk. So they hired some men to get rid of him.

"One morning Master Chen was walking along the dockyards carrying a tube. With his head in the clouds, he did not notice the motorcycle coming towards him. A man on the back of the motorcycle pointed his tommy gun. With one long blast, he sent Master Chen to the Other World.

"I was sixteen and working in the pharmacy warehouse. When I saw the nose of the gun, I instantly dove behind some boxes. I heard the tac tac tac tac tac tac and saw the snout of the smoking weapon and the blood on Master Chen's robe as he collapsed. I watched the tube roll slowly toward me and stop where I was crouching. During those troubled times, the authorities did not get too involved in that type of situation. The police simply came to wrap up the body and the municipal van took it to the Nanshi bridge on the other side of the river. The affair ended there.

"I looked inside the tube and discovered a *hua* of Master Chen. I took the tube back to my boss's house, the late father of the present Mr. Ha. I hid it in the cellar under buckets of rubble and slabs of coal. Soon after, I was enlisted into the Liberation Army, where I served twelve years. When I returned, Mr. Ha's son found me a job at the people's hotel. I have lived near the Ha family ever since. After all these years, I had almost forgotten." As he finished his story, *Yeye* Tchou gave a great sigh.

I could not stand the idea that the spirit of Master Chen had been roaming the street for so long, unable to have any rest. His family did not know how his life had really ended. Because his body was never recovered, his family was unable to perform a correct burial, and, therefore, his soul could not rest. He needed to be honored by his sons as the dead should be honored by the living. I knew I had to do justice to the soul of Master Chen and inform his family.

Yi, *Yeye* Tchou and I spent the rest of the afternoon digging in the Ha family's store of coal with shovels and buckets to find the tube. When we found it, I hurried home. I was very late. When she hugged me, *Mama's* heart beat like the wings of a bird in a cage. After I told her the story, *Mama* was proud of how brave I had been and about my decision to bring honor to Master Chen by writing a *xin* to his family.

★   ★   ★

So now I have a long *xin* to write to Master Chen's son telling him the story of his father's death. I smile at the *hua* of my *gui*, finally recovered after all these years from the Ha family's coal cellar and soon to be returned to his family. I feel a small pain behind my ear which makes me close my eyes.

"Goodbye, *xiao* Li," whispers Master Chen. "And thank you!"

I open my eyes. *Mama,* seated at her sewing machine, pulls on the spool, and unrolls a blue swatch of cloth. And I begin my *xin*.

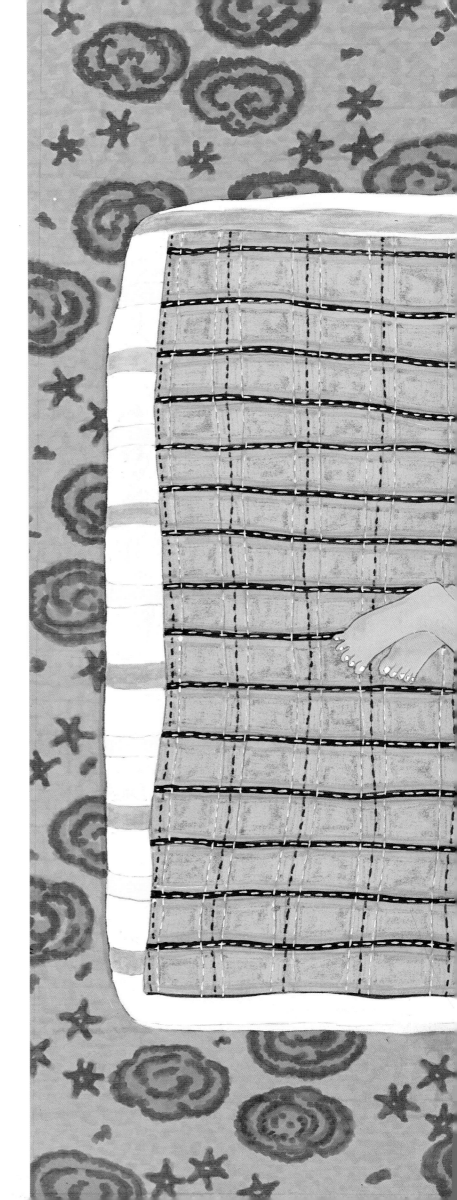

Author and Artist Note

The Ghost of Shanghai is set in contemporary China, in and around Shanghai, the country's largest and most modern industrial city. China is a large country made up of many different provinces, religions, and dialects. The main Chinese dialect, Mandarin, is used in the story. Li, the story's heroine, has grown up in the 1990s. Her parents and neighbors have lived through some very difficult periods in Chinese history. Their past has shaped the climate she lives in, and has influenced the interaction she has with them and her *gui,* Master Chen.

For thousands of years, China was ruled by many different dynasties. The last dynasty, the Ch-ing, ended in 1912. After that time, the country was faced with many social and political changes. By the end of World War II, China was divided into two main political parties: the Nationalists, led by Chiang Kai-shek, and the Communists, led by Mao Tsetung. The two sides fought for control of the country for many years. In 1949, the People's Republic of China was formed with the Communists taking control and thus establishing Mao as the leader of mainland China.

Mao created new economic, social, and political programs, but many of these programs caused problems. The Great Leap Forward in 1958 was a program aimed at making the country a major industrial power, but instead it caused economic recession. In the Cultural Revolution, which took place from 1966–76, Mao closed many of the colleges and universities in order to enforce his singular way of thinking, which often did not allow teachers to speak their minds and which repressed creative thought. Many people died during this period, and the country suffered major economic problems. Today the Cultural Revolution is still a presence in the minds of the Chinese, and is regarded as a sad time in China's history. Mrs. Suzu, Li's neighbor, was a young woman during the Cultural Revolution. Because she grew up with great hardship, it is hard for her to accept the country's recent changes and the easier times such wealthy families as the Has have enjoyed.

After Mao died in 1976, Deng Xiaoping eventually took over with the goal of instituting economic and political reforms. In 1989, student protesters, who felt that not enough social reforms were being implemented, held a series of demonstrations that culminated in a violent suppression by the Chinese army at Tiananmen Square. Even so, China today has seen many economic reforms and western influences have crept in, especially in the large cities like Shanghai. This is apparent in what Li sees in the house of the Ha family. Downtown Shanghai and the Ha residence are filled with luxuries and exotic objects that Li's family does not have.

There are also socio-economic differences between *Yeye* Tchou and the Ha family. *Yeye* Tchou and Master Chen, who grew up in the earlier part of the century, also experienced the difficult periods in Chinese history. Not only did they live through such Communist programs as the Great Leap Forward and the Cultural Revolution, but they were also affected by China's troubles before Mao took over. As *Yeye* Tchou explains in the story, he participated in many of the conflicts between the Nationalists and the Communists before the Republic was established. His life has been characterized by strife, and he has never experienced the sort of ease that recent economic reform has allowed people like the present Ha family.

Through the story and art, we hope that children may come to understand how people (especially children) live in China today, and that they appreciate the importance of justice and honor.

Glossary

CHINESE (MANDARIN) WORD:	ENGLISH TRANSLATION:	PRONOUNCIATION:
baba	father	bah·bah
bowuguan	museum	b'wō·woo·gwan
didi	younger brother	dē·dē
gongchang	factory	gung·chăng
gui	ghost	gwā
hua	painting	hwah
kuai	a monetary unit	kwī
lifu	formal dress(es)	lē·foo
mama	mother	mah·mah
nuer	daughter	nü'er
shuijiao	dumplings	shwā·jē·ow
xiao	little	s'yow
xiao peng you	little friend	s'yow·pun·yō
xin	letter	sēn
yeye	grandfather	yĕ·yĕ
zixingche	bicycle	z·sing·chŭ

Editor, English-language edition: Lia Ronnen
Design Coordinator, English-language edition: Ellen Friedman

Library of Congress Cataloging-in-Publication Data
Guillot, Claude
The ghost of Shanghai / Claude Guillot : illustrated by Fabienne Burckel.
p. cm.
Summary: In Shanghai, Li has a bicycle accident, goes through a near-death experience, and meets the ghost of
Master Chen, whom she decides to honor by performing an important task for him.
ISBN 0–8109–4129–5

[1. Ghosts—Fiction. 2. Near-death experiences—Fiction.
3. Shanghai (China)—Fiction. 4. China—Fiction.] I. Burckel,
Fabienne, ill. II. Title
PZ7.G9388Gh 1999
[E]—dc21   98-52764

Harry N. Abrams, Inc.
100 Fifth Avenue
New York, N.Y. 10011
www.abramsbooks.com